If You're Afraid of the Dark
Remember the Night Rainbow

by Cooper Edens

THE GREEN TIGER PRESS

Calligraphy by
George Weinberg-Harter

Words & Pictures Copyright © 1979
by Cooper Edens

3rd Edition

Paperbound ISBN 0-88138-044-X
19 20

If tomorrow morning
the sky falls...

have clouds
  for breakfast,

∾

If night falls...

use stars
for streetlights.

～

If the moon gets
stuck in a tree...

cover the hole
in the sky with
a strawberry.

~~

If you have butterflies
in your stomach ...

ask them into
your heart.

～

If your heart catches
in your throat...

ask a bird
how she sings.

～

If the birds
forget their songs...

listen to
a pebble
instead.

~

If you lose
a memory...

embroider
a new one to
take its place.

If you lose the key...

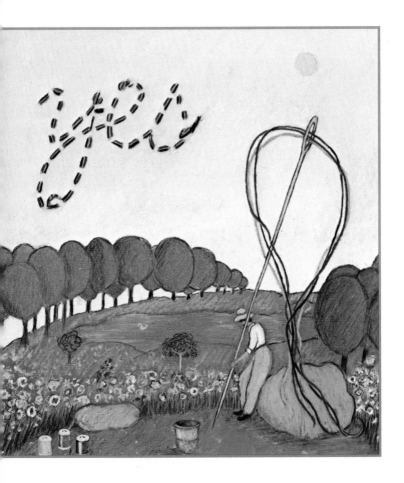

throw away
the house.

~~~

If the clock stops...

use your own hands
to tell time.

~~

If the light goes out...

wear it around
your neck and
go dancing.

~

If the bus doesn't come...

catch a fast cloud.

~

If it's the last dance...

dance backwards,

~~~

If you find your
socks don't match ...

stand in a
Flowerbed.

～

If your shoes don't fit...

give them to the fish
in the pond.

~~~

If your horse needs shoes...

let him use his wings.

~

If the sun
never shines again...

hold fireflies
in your hands
to keep warm.

~

If you're afraid
of the dark ...

remember the
night rainbow.

~~~

If there is no
happy ending...

make one out of
cookie dough.

Color Separation by
Sunset Graphics, San Diego, California
and
Photolitho AG, Gossau, Switzerland
Printed & bound in Hong Kong